Ballerina
Jade and the Carnival

Welcome to the world of Enchantia!

I have always loved to dance. The captivating
music and wonderful stories of ballet are so
inspiring. So come with me and let's follow
Jade on her magical adventures in
Enchantia, where the stories of dance will
take you on a very special journey.

[signature]

p.s. Turn to the back to learn a special
dance step from me...

First publishe
HarperCollins *Children's Books* is a division of HarperCollins *Publishers* Ltd,
77-85 Fulham Palace Road, Hammersmith, London W6 8JB

The HarperCollins website address is
www.harpercollins.co.uk

1

Text copyright © HarperCollins *Children's Books* 2010
Illustrations by Dynamo Limited
Illustrations copyright © HarperCollins *Children's Books* 2010

MAGIC BALLERINA™ and the 'Magic Ballerina' logo are
trademarks of HarperCollins Publishers Ltd.

ISBN13 978 0 00 734878 7

Printed and bound in England by
Clays Ltd, St Ives plc

Magic Ballerina
Jade and the Carnival

Darcey Bussell

HarperCollins *Children's Books*

To Phoebe and Zoe, as they are the inspiration
behind Magic Ballerina.

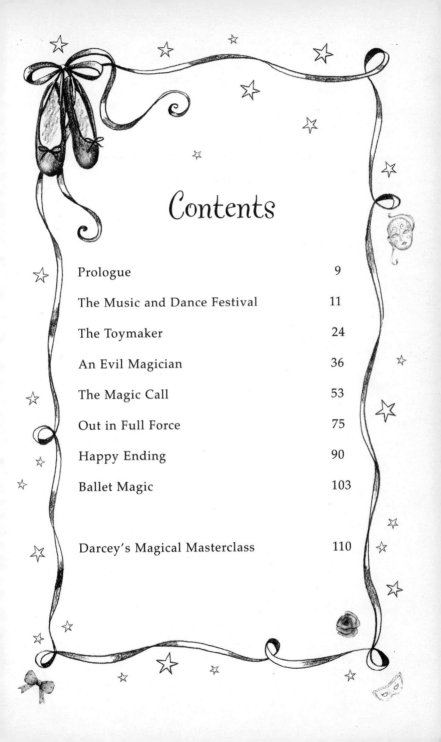

Contents

Prologue

*In the soft, pale light, the girl stood
with her head bent and her hands
held lightly in front of her.
There was a moment's silence and then
the first notes of the music began.
For as long as the girl could remember
music had seemed to tell her of
another world – a magical, exciting
world – that lay far, far away.
She always felt if she could just
close her eyes and lose herself,
then she would get there.
Maybe this time. As the music
swirled inside her, she swept
her arms above her head, rose on to
her toes and began to dance…*

The Music and Dance Festival

Jade had finished her lunch, but she couldn't bring herself to ask to leave the table – not when her family were chatting about the Music and Dance Festival. It was going to be held just round the corner from them and Jade couldn't wait.

"It's so exciting!" said Lottie, one of her little sisters.

"Mummy's said we can help on the cake stall, didn't you, Mummy?" added Hannah, the other one.

Jade's mum smiled as her dad turned to her little brothers. "You two rebels are helping me with the hoops game, you know!"

The twins bounced up and down in their seats, asking questions about their 'special jobs,' and how much money they'd be allowed to spend, while Jade

drifted off into a daydream.

It was really wonderful that the festival was taking place so close. It made Jade feel extra specially connected to it. She'd already worked out a dance for her ballet class to do, and was sure that her teacher, Madame Za-Za, would help her teach it to everyone. She started to imagine performing the dance and how all the audience would clap loudly at the end. But a moment later she shot out of her daydream at the sound of her mum's voice.

"Jade! You're going to be late for your rehearsal!"

Jade leaped up from the table and rushed off to get her ballet bag. It was all packed and ready apart from her red ballet shoes, which she kept in her room. Running upstairs she felt another rush of excitement. She was about to go to the

first practice for the festival. Going to
Madame Za-Za's twice in a day was a
real treat, because Jade loved dancing
more than anything in the world.

She tucked her
precious red shoes
in her bag and
thought about how

lucky she was to own them. They were so
special – not just because so many
brilliant ballerinas had worn them before
her, but because the shoes were magic
too! They had the power to take her to the
Land of Enchantia where all the characters
from the ballets lived. Jade had already

been there, and each time she'd had the most incredible adventure.

"Right," said Madame Za-Za, clapping her hands to hush the excitement as she looked round the class with shining eyes. "Now that I've explained about the Music and Dance Festival, it only remains for me to tell you about *your* role in the dancing!"

"I've got a good idea!" Chloe called out.

"Me too!" said Amber.

Jade couldn't believe it when lots of

other girls chimed in that they had ideas as well. This wasn't what she had been expecting at all.

"Well, that is good," said Madame Za-Za, bringing the silence back as she spoke, "because I think it best that you dance what *you* want to dance. It should be fun. So get into small groups and start work straight away. I'll come round and help where needed."

"But… but… excuse me, Madame Za-Za…"

Jade quickly interrupted, feeling her heart beat faster. She really wanted everyone to dance *her* dance.

"I've been… reading about the ballet *Petrouchka*, and I've watched the DVD too, and it's really great. It's given me an

idea for a character dance with light-hearted characters like clowns because Petrouchka is a puppet clown…"

Jade faded out. She could tell that the others didn't think much of her idea, and even Madame Za-Za was looking a bit doubtful.

"I've never heard of *Petrouchka*!" Amy said.

"That's no problem, I can teach you!" Jade answered quickly. "I thought a character dance would be really cool for an outdoor festival. We could dress up in brightly coloured costumes and even wear silly red noses," she added. Then she stopped talking and looked round hopefully, but the rest of the class didn't appear at all interested. A few of them were looking down or even pulling faces.

"I don't want to do a clown dance," one of the girls said quietly.

"I don't think I'd be much good at it," someone else said.

"Me neither," came a general chorus.

"All right," said Madame Za-Za. "Then we'll stick to what I said originally and all work out our own dances in small groups. Now, off you go!"

A big wave of disappointment came over Jade. She'd been hoping that the

class would all want to dance together.
And she'd been sure that Madame Za-Za
would let her teach everyone the clown
dance, but now it looked as though she
would be dancing it on her own. Sighing
with frustration, she looked round.
Already everyone was practising their
dances, and Madame Za-Za
was at the other side of
the room helping one
of the groups. No one
noticed Jade slipping
out of the studio.

The corridor felt quiet
and cool, and Jade stood

still, trying to calm down and think what
to do. Maybe she ought to join one of the
groups?

But her own dance was so special to
her. She stood in the opening position,
her supporting leg
in a *demi-plié*,
then stretched
her left foot out
behind her. She
gasped.

Her shoe was
glowing. Yes, and so
was the other one! And now she was
surrounded by swirling colours that were

lifting her up and spinning her round. Her heart raced. Was she being whisked away to Enchantia?

The Toymaker

As soon as Jade's feet touched the ground, she felt excitement mounting inside her. It looked as though she'd stepped right into the middle of a wonderful carnival in Enchantia. What a coincidence when she'd only just been

practising for her own local music and
dance festival! This one was much bigger
and grander, though.

Jade was standing in a wide avenue full
of brightly coloured stalls. The soldiers
from the *Nutcracker* ballet were marching

down the street and there were people
lining the avenue, clapping as they
passed. Behind them came a group of
clog dancers.

Laughter, music and cheering filled the
air. And that wasn't all. Where was that
delicious toffee-apple smell coming
from? Jade followed her nose to try and
track it down, but couldn't help stopping
every so often to see what lovely trinkets,
jewels and accessories the stalls held.

Everyone was smiley and happy, except
one person just ahead who looked very
downcast. He was wearing a checked
shirt and a leather waistcoat, dark

coloured trousers that came to just below the knee and a spotty scarf tied loosely around his neck.

I wonder what's making him so sad, thought Jade. Her hand suddenly flew to her mouth as she'd realised who was standing beside the dejected-looking man. It was her old friend, the White Cat. In

her excitement at the magnificent
carnival, she'd completely forgotten that
the White Cat usually came to greet her
when she arrived in Enchantia.

"White Cat! Hello!" she called,
threading her way through the crowd.

He looked up and smiled. "Jade! I was
expecting you!" The White Cat hugged
her then introduced her to his unhappy
friend. "This is Leonardo, the toymaker."

"Hello, Leonardo," Jade smiled,
reaching out to shake his hand.

"Hello," Leonardo smiled gently, but he
still looked so sad. Jade looked to the
White Cat expectantly.

"Leonardo's precious puppet Peter has been stolen and put under someone else's spell," the White Cat explained.

Jade gasped. "Do you mean… Peter, the clown from the ballet *Petrouchka*?" she asked.

29

Leonardo nodded forlornly and through Jade's head flashed a series of pictures of the three puppets from the ballet – the soldier with his sword, the ballerina with her porcelain face and round blue eyes, and Petrouchka, the clown – Peter for short – with his baggy trousers and friendly smile.

"Peter has been helping me in my shop ever since I first made him," explained Leonardo in a thin voice. "And I miss him terribly. He's like a son to me because, although he looks like an ordinary puppet, he has a heart and can feel things." Leonardo's head dropped. "I can't bear to lose him like this."

"I'm so sorry," said Jade softly. "Have you any idea where to look for him?"

The White Cat pointed to a little theatre nearby. "He's right there! In the puppet show!"

Jade followed the White Cat's gaze and her eyes flew wide open in surprise. "So why can't you just go and get him?"

Leonardo sighed. "That's exactly what we thought. Only now that Peter's under someone's spell, he simply doesn't know me any more," Leonardo finished dejectedly. "Look… you'll see…"

He called out to Peter in a sing-song voice and waved cheerfully.

The puppet glanced over fleetingly, but his eyes were completely blank. Then he carried on entertaining the crowd, who chuckled and cheered at his antics. They

seemed to like him more than any of the
other puppets.

"But surely people recognise him," said
Jade, feeling bewildered.

Leonardo shook his
head. "Peter's very shy.
He always stays in the
workshop at the back if
there are customers in the shop. The
audience here are just enjoying the show.
They don't realise that anything is wrong.
But the trouble is…" Poor Leonardo was
close to tears, "…if Peter doesn't come
back to me he'll eventually lose his heart
and become just an ordinary puppet."

"That's terrible!" said Jade. "We have to find out who's done this!"

The White Cat put a soft paw on the arm of the toymaker. "Try not to worry, Leonardo," he said. "Go back and look after your shop. Jade and I will come here again later and see who collects Peter.

There's nothing we can do until then."

"Yes, the White Cat and I will make sure you get Peter back," added Jade. But the moment the words were out of her mouth she wished she hadn't said them. How could they possibly get Peter back if he was under someone's magic spell and didn't even recognise his owner?

An Evil Magican

Jade and the White Cat walked despondently around the carnival, heads down, worrying about Peter and Leonardo.

"There's nothing we can do until later, so we might as well at least *try* to enjoy ourselves," said the White Cat after a while.

Jade knew he was right. "OK," she said as they passed a game of skittles. "Then why don't we have a go at this!"

The White Cat turned out to be very good at the game and won a fine rosette which he stuck to his hat. Then Jade ate some candyfloss and together they watched the acrobats and jugglers. After that they joined in with some lively folk dancing in the big village square, but even doing such fun things couldn't put the thought of Peter out of their minds.

And eventually, they noticed one or two of the stall holders packing away for the day and thought it was time to go

back and see if the puppet show was
coming to an end.

Jade's footsteps quickened.

"We must be careful, Jade," the White
Cat warned, hurrying along just behind
her. "If someone comes to collect Peter
we mustn't let them see us. It might be
King Rat!" His voice shook slightly on
the last two words.

Jade had been thinking exactly that.
She shivered at the thought of the other
evil characters of Enchantia she knew
about – the Dark Witch and the Wicked
Fairy. It would be awful if one of them
had put a spell on Peter. Their magic was

so powerful.

"We're nearly there," said the White Cat, slowing his pace and speaking quietly.

Jade looked around, her eyes widening. Where was the puppet theatre? She turned in panic to the White Cat. "It's gone! Oh no! We're too late! Peter's been taken!"

"Ssh," whispered the cat. "Look…"

Jade followed his gaze. Wandering along a little further ahead, was a small figure. Peter!

"Come on!" said Jade to her friend. "Let's stop him."

"No, wait," the White Cat cautioned Jade. "We mustn't go rushing in. It's best

to be patient and find out where he's going first. Besides," he added, "the person who put a spell on him might be anywhere around. We must keep ourselves hidden."

Jade nodded. She knew the White Cat was right, so together they began to follow Peter, keeping their distance.

"Look!" said Jade, after a few minutes. "He's about to go into that little cottage. We've got to talk to him!" She rushed forward, ignoring the White Cat's attempts to stop her. "Peter! Peter! You don't have to go in here. You don't belong here. Remember Leonardo? He's missing you terribly, Peter. Just come with me now and I'll take you back to him, I promise."

But Peter just stared at Jade blankly then let himself into the cottage. Jade watched in dismay, and all the energy left her body when she heard the key turn on the other side of the door. Peter was locking himself in.

"He really *is* under someone else's spell," she said with a hopeless sigh. She felt a paw on her shoulder. "Oh, White Cat, what are we going to do now?"

At that moment there came a loud hoot of laughter from somewhere above and a monstrous owl flew over them, its wings spread wide.

"Oh, my shimmering whiskers!" exclaimed the White Cat. "Von Rotbart!"

Von Rotbart? Jade had heard that name before. "Isn't he the evil magician who put a spell on the swans in *Swan Lake*?" She didn't wait for an answer. "Yes," she breathed. "I remember, he sometimes appears in the form of an owl, doesn't he?"

But the White Cat didn't answer. "Oh, my glittering tail!" he murmured instead, staring into the distance, his faced pinched in a frown. "Now we know who is responsible for putting the spell on Peter. But what can we do to stop it?"

Jade nodded as the realisation dawned on her of the task that lay ahead. "We must follow him," she decided.

The White Cat was already drawing a circle on the ground with his tail. Jade stepped inside the ring of sparkles as it started to spin. After a moment she and the White Cat were lifted up and whisked away.

"It's so beautiful!" said Jade, staring round as soon as they alighted by a lake. "And… quiet."

Shafts of sunlight were slanting

through the dark trees surrounding them, sending glittering trails across the still dark water. On the other side of the lake, shadowy white shapes moved amongst the trees and Jade caught her breath. These were the swans. She'd already met two of them, Sabrina and Sahara, who had rescued her and the White Cat from the Wicked Fairy's tower once before.

"Do you think Von Rotbart is hiding in the trees?" whispered Jade with a shiver.

The White Cat didn't reply, but his eyes narrowed as he stared into the depths of the forest. "The trouble with Von Rotbart," he said slowly, his gaze never

leaving the trees, "is that his magic powers are so strong, he can give himself either appearance he wants. Man or owl."

Jade scanned the sky fearfully, but only saw a few small birds in the distance. "I don't think—"

Her words were stifled by a gasp. A tall, thin man wearing a heavy cloak of dark feathers was emerging from deep in the forest, walking purposefully towards them. As he drew nearer, Jade felt her heart hammering. His face was shaped like an owl's with enormous round staring eyes.

"Ha! I was expecting you two

meddlers. Well, you needn't have bothered to come here, because the puppet is no longer anything to do with anyone except  me. I've removed him from the other puppets. He was wasted in that show and in that little cottage."

"Wasted?" Jade questioned. "What do you mean?"

"That doesn't matter." Von Rotbart grinned maliciously. "The important thing is that he's being put to far better use than

ever before. He works for *me* now and
will never return to the silly toymaker.
He's *my* assistant. He obeys my *every*
command! In fact, he has entirely
forgotten about Leonardo and his life
before!"

Jade and the White Cat exchanged a
look of horror. Then before their eyes,
great wings sprouted from Von Rotbart's

body and began to spread wider and wider. The cloak slid from his shoulders and dissolved on the ground as he became entirely covered in feathers.

"I command you to go! Leave my territory! You're not welcome here," came a threatening screech.

Then with a beating of wings the monstrous owl rose into the air, hooting

tauntingly as he crossed high over the
lake and disappeared back into the dark
trees.

The Magic Call

"Whatever are we going to do, White Cat?" asked Jade in a small voice, once the echo of the owl hoots had faded. She and the White Cat began to walk towards the lake.

The White Cat frowned. "Good

question. And here's another one. How do you rescue someone when you haven't a clue where they are, and even if you did know, you *couldn't* rescue them because they don't *want* to be rescued?"

A feeling of complete hopelessness was creeping around Jade. "He told us to go away, but we can't do that. It would feel like deserting Peter. We've got to find out where Von Rotbart has taken him."

As her friend nodded and frowned thoughtfully, Jade noticed that the white shapes of the swans were clearer now. They had clustered round the other side of the lake at the water's edge.

"Shall we go and see if Sahara and Sabrina are amongst them?" asked Jade, moving closer to the edge of the water. "They might know where Von Rotbart has hidden Peter."

The White Cat nodded again, but Jade could tell he was anxious about something.

She looked at him carefully. "Are you worried that Von Rotbart might be angry if he notices we haven't obeyed his command?"

"Not exactly," the White Cat replied. "It's just that—"

Jade didn't discover what he was going to say because a sharp gust of wind made her lose her balance and she almost knocked the White Cat over.

"Wh…what was that? How can it be so calm one minute and so windy the next?"

The White Cat began to say something in reply, but the noise of the leaves and twigs rustling on the forest floor, drowned out his voice. Then the branches of the trees began to creak and Jade saw the gigantic owl swooping low over the lake towards them, the tips of his talons shooting a powerful arc of water up into the air.

"What's happening!" cried Jade.

The owl was so close that she could see his angry eyes.

"How dare you disobey me!" he cawed.

Jade and the White Cat clung to each other and a second later they found themselves hurtling through the air, trapped in the sharp talons of the owl.

"Oh, my shimmering whiskers and glittering tail!" the White Cat cried. "He's carrying us away over the lake!"

Jade could only just make out his next words as the wind rushed past her ears.

"I'm scared of water!" the White Cat cried as his rosette fell from his hat.

The owl laughed cruelly. "What an unfortunate feline! Well, you're about to make a splash."

And suddenly the sharp talons were no longer holding on to Jade and she and the White Cat were falling, as if in slow motion, towards the dark lake.

"Help!" called the White Cat. Jade

closed her eyes and waited to hit the cold water. She knew she could swim to the side and save herself, but what about the White Cat? Did she have the strength to save her dear friend too?

But a soft, clear voice rose up from the lake. "We will protect you. Don't worry!"

At first Jade thought she must have imagined it. But then she felt herself cushioned by something that looked like an enormous white feather duvet floating in the middle of the lake. The White Cat was beside her.

"It's the swans! They've saved us!"

"Sahara! Sabrina! This is wonderful!"

The White Cat's voice was filled with gratitude.

"We guessed that Von Rotbart might have something evil planned when we saw him talking to you amongst the trees," said Sahara, in her quiet strong voice. "So when we saw him swooping down towards you just now, we knew for certain what he intended. So we all swam out here together to catch you."

"We're grateful to every single one of you," said Jade, gently laying her head against Sahara's neck.

"Yes, thank you so much," added the White Cat, who still looked a bit grey in the face from the shock. Then he turned to Jade. "But now we really must be going!"

Jade nodded and quickly explained to the swans that she and the White Cat were on a mission to find Peter the puppet, who had been stolen from his owner by Von Rotbart.

"But where do you find a puppet in the whole of Enchantia?" she sighed helplessly, as the White Cat caught hold of his tail ready to swish it in a magic circle.

"Maybe you need to find the puppet's heart first," said Sahara in a voice as gentle as the breeze that rippled the lake.

Jade was puzzled by this, but there was no time to think about it now. "Thank you all, again!" she cried, stepping carefully into the ring of silver sparks that floated off the backs of the white swans. "Goodbye!"

Jade's feet landed in the midst of the carnival with the echo of Sahara's words in her head. *Maybe you need to find the puppet's heart first.*

"That's it!" she said, her eyes lighting up.

"What?" asked the White Cat.

"We've got to somehow get to Peter's little heart."

The White Cat turned sharply, as if eager to latch on to whatever Jade was trying to work out. He spoke briskly and encouragingly. "Uh-huh, uh-huh… Go on."

"You remember the time when we were imprisoned in the Wicked Fairy's high tower and I used the power of dance to summon Sahara and Sabrina?" Jade said, a new feeling of hope springing up inside her.

The White Cat nodded.

"Well, perhaps if I do Peter's dance and think about him at the same time, I'll be able to summon him too!" she finished.

"Y… yes… maybe," agreed the White Cat. But he was frowning, and didn't seem at all sure.

"What is it, Cat? Don't you think it would work?"

The White Cat pursed his lips thoughtfully. "I know that it's worked for us before, but the trouble is, Von Rotbart's magic is much more powerful than the Wicked Fairy's. I'm just not sure that one person dancing Peter's dance and

thinking about him would be enough to
break such a strong spell."

Jade felt a sigh rising up inside her, but
it faded almost immediately as the most
brilliant idea popped into her head. She
turned back to her friend and spoke in a
rush. "Well, would it work if we all

danced Peter's dance together? I mean every single person at the carnival?"

Jade looked round and the White Cat's gaze followed. There was a different atmosphere now because the day time had slipped into a warm evening, made even brighter by the coloured lights that were sparkling like stars all over the place. There seemed to be more people than ever out enjoying themselves.

"It's worth a try," said the White Cat, pondering the idea. "Yes, I think it could work."

"Good!" Jade hurried on. "Because I know the dance – so I can teach

everyone! We just need to get the people to stop what they're doing and join in. We'll go round and explain to everyone about poor Peter being stolen," she added, sticking her chin up.

There was a doubtful look lurking in the White Cat's eyes, but he nodded and tried to smile. "Let's get started then. There's no time like the present!"

So after agreeing to meet up in twenty minutes back at the same place, they went their separate ways.

Jade was eager to get started. Rushing up to a line of people queuing to see a fortune teller, she cleared her throat and clapped her hands. "Excuse me, but I wanted to tell you about Leonardo, the toymaker. Something very sad has happened. His little puppet, Peter the clown has been stolen."

A murmur ran through the queue. "Oh dear, that's terrible!"

"Yes," Jade quickly went on, "and we have to get him back, but he's had a spell put on him…"

"A spell!" said the people nearest Jade.

But the ones who were at the front of the queue weren't really listening any more because they were getting ready to talk to the fortune teller.

Jade raised her voice slightly and spoke urgently. "We need to break the spell. We have to learn Peter's dance."

But everyone was so distracted that they weren't really listening.

"It's quite easy to learn," she went on brightly. "I can teach you all…"

But no one was paying her any attention, and in the end Jade wandered dejectedly off to find another group of people.

For the next twenty minutes it was the same story. Whoever she spoke to seemed shocked and sorry for Leonardo and Peter, but then they became distracted by something else at the carnival. It was just no good.

"How did you get on?" Jade asked her friend, the moment they met up. But she knew from his face what his answer would be.

"No good, I'm afraid."

"Me neither."

Out of the corner of her eye, Jade could see Leonardo coming towards them, and felt a glimmer of hope until she saw that he had a tear in his eye.

"Peter hasn't returned," he said in a forlorn voice.

Jade bit her lip. There just had to be
something they could do.

Out in Full Force!

Leonardo sat down on a little podium just behind them, as though he was too weak with grief to stand for a moment longer. The White Cat sat down beside him.

"Try not to worry, Leonardo… I'm sure we'll think of something."

And as Jade looked at the White Cat
and the toymaker sitting there, an idea
jumped into her mind.

"That's it!" she said, clapping her
hands together.

The White Cat
looked up hopefully
at the sight of
Jade, performing
a *développé*.
Even Leonardo
managed a
smile.

"What?" they
asked together.

"Look where you two are sitting!" said Jade. "Isn't it a perfect little stage for the two of us to dance on, White Cat? The dancers from this afternoon have gone. And now it's our turn. Let's see if we can attract a crowd that way!"

The White Cat was puzzled. "A crowd? You mean *we're* going to be entertainers?"

"Yes!" cried Jade. "That's the way to attract people, isn't it?" she laughed.

It took a moment for the White Cat to realise what Jade meant, then he leaped

up and performed a perfect *pas de chat* in
the middle of the podium. He was
grinning his head off.

Jade and the Carnival

"Good thinking! Good thinking!" said
Leonardo, happier than he'd sounded for
a long time. "I shall be the first member
of your audience!"

"Hang on a sec, what are we going to
dance?" asked the White Cat.

"Peter's dance, of course!" replied Jade
in a flash. "You play the part of the owner
and I'll be Petrouchka!"

It felt good to be dancing on the little
stage with the White Cat. They didn't
need to work anything out, just danced
from their hearts and tried to tell the story
through mime and expression.

In no time at all a few people had

79

joined Leonardo and gradually a little
crowd started to form. They began to clap
in time, which attracted even more people
who might have walked straight past if
they hadn't heard the applause.

Over the next few minutes more and more people came to watch Jade and the White Cat, as they spun and wove the emotional story through their dance. At the end there was loud applause and

cheering, which drew an even greater crowd. Everyone wanted to know what was happening. Jade couldn't help feeling excited. Her plan was working. Now all she had to do was make her announcement.

The moment the final claps and cheers melted away, she began to speak, clearly and strongly, explaining how Peter the clown had been cruelly stolen from Leonardo and put under an evil spell. And as her tale unfolded, she felt wrapped up in the sympathy of the crowd. They seemed outraged by what had happened.

"I need your help," Jade said finally,

speaking passionately. "If we all dance Peter's dance together and think about him at the same time, then maybe we can draw him back."

Immediately the White Cat bowed dramatically to Jade, removing his hat and sweeping it low before tossing it in the air. A gasp rushed through the crowd as the hat landed perfectly back on the White Cat's head. Then the dancing began.

It was absolutely wonderful to see so many people having fun as they learned the dance. Jade worked hard to make sure

everyone could master the jerky
movements and scissor jumps in the
clown's dance, as well as the softer arm
stretches. She felt sorry to see that
Leonardo was the only person standing
quite still, but it was easy to understand
why. His face wore a tense look as he
strained to see over the heads of the
crowd. He must have been desperately
hoping that his precious Peter might
suddenly appear.

But so far, it wasn't happening, and
small pinpricks of worry broke out all
over Jade. What if he never appeared?
What if she was wrong and it wouldn't be

enough to break the enchantment, simply by having everyone dancing together? What if she was wasting everyone's time?

Jade told herself off for losing concentration. She must try harder. But she was starting to get tired. Out of the corner of her eye she noticed Leonardo hurrying off in the direction of his shop.

When he returned, head down, footsteps dragging, a few minutes later, Jade knew that Peter couldn't have returned. How could she have ever thought that more people dancing would be enough to break a spell by a powerful owl magician? She looked across at the

White Cat in despair, but her friend's eyes were twinkling…

Jade followed his gaze and she saw with delight that the Sweets had arrived at the Carnival. And then the Fairies were there too, sending bright arcs of glitter through the air as they danced.

Jade felt a new spring in her step.

"Look over here!" came the voice of the White Cat.

Something in his tone brought a new surge of hope and Jade turned to see what her friend had seen. Even more people were joining in, smiling and laughing, dancing from their hearts. It brought a magic to her feet, which raced through her whole body.

And who was that, joining the Fairies at the back, their tiaras and crowns sparkling brightly? Jade gasped. It was King Tristan and Queen Isabella, Prince Florimund and Princess Aurelia,

Cinderella and Prince Charming. The royalty of Enchantia had come to dance too!

Happy Ending

Would Jade's plan work? She held her breath hopefully. Absolutely everyone in Enchantia was dancing Peter's dance, but nothing seemed to be happening. Then Jade realised that there was still one person who was too forlorn to dance. She

went to the edge of the podium and reached out her hand.

"Come and join me, Leonardo!" she said softly.

Leonardo dipped his head sadly. "I'm… not sure."

But Jade reached out even further and managed to grasp his hand.

The toymaker sighed and stepped up on to the podium, which instantly made everyone clap. He waved a hand to say thank you, then as Jade put everything she had into her dance, Leonardo clapped in time and began tapping his foot. Amazingly, after a minute or two, his body began to move in time with the music too and his face lit up.

It was at that moment when there came a bird-like shriek of horror from above. It pierced the air and made everyone stop dancing and look up.

A gasp went through the crowd at the sight of a giant owl disappearing into the distance. Jade felt something truly magical as she looked down at the people. She exchanged the briefest look with the White Cat. His eyes said, *The spell is broken!*

But where was Peter?

Then something began to happen. The crowd seemed to be shifting slightly and parting. They were pressing themselves back to make a way through the middle. Jade felt a lump in her throat. Leonardo must have caught something in her expression, because he was leaning forwards, his eyes searching the sea of faces below.

"Peter!" he whispered in a voice that cracked with emotion.

Then as the people broke into applause, the clown puppet in his baggy trousers made his way through the crowd. After a few seconds everyone fell silent, watching, waiting. Peter drew nearer to the podium and Jade noticed tears in Leonardo's eyes as he stretched out his arms to his puppet child.

"I lost you!" came Peter's small lilting voice, breaking the silence. "But I'm back now!"

Then Leonardo lifted his beloved
puppet on to the podium and hugged him
tight.

A few moments later the White Cat raised his voice. All eyes were upon him.

"We have Jade to thank for this happy ending!" he said. "She got everyone to dance, drawing Peter back to us. Let's show our thanks!"

Another thunderous wave of applause filled the air, making Jade burst with pride. But she too raised her hand for silence. "I couldn't have done it without all of you, and I thank you on behalf of Leonardo—"

"And on behalf of me!" chimed in Peter, which made everyone laugh.

Then he began to dance himself, so Jade and the White Cat stepped down from the podium and moved into the audience, while Leonardo stayed beside Peter and clapped to the beat.

"They're having such fun!" said Jade to the White Cat some time later when the carnival was back in full swing. They were watching Peter and Leonardo going up and down on magnificent horses on the magic carousel.

"Let's join them!" suggested the White Cat, once the carousel had slowed down to let more people on. Jade laughed happily as she climbed on to a beautiful silver horse with a golden bridle and the

White Cat mounted a black horse beside her.

Leonardo and Peter stayed on the carousel for another turn and the swirling music grew louder as the horses started to

rise and fall again. Whirling around, Jade felt dizzy with happiness and it was no surprise when tingles started up in the tips of her toes.

But when the tingles began to grow stronger she stuck her leg out to the side. And it was a shock to see her red shoe glowing brightly. Surely she couldn't be leaving Enchantia in the middle of a carousel ride?

"White Cat!" she hissed, nodding at her shoe.

"Oh, my glimmering tail!" exclaimed the White Cat, his eyes wide with amazement. "High five!" He raised a paw and leaned out from his horse.

Jade laughed and clapped her friend's paw happily.

"Thank you, Jade!" said the White Cat,

his eyes serious. "The power of your personality pulled that crowd in and everyone dancing together really broke the spell!"

Jade nodded hard. "Thank you, White Cat," she smiled. "I'm so happy that it worked." Suddenly, she felt lighter than she had for a long time and knew the moment to go was almost upon her. "Goodbye! Goodbye!"

"Goodbye Jade!"

And with that, the colours of the carousel blended into the colours that were swirling around and Jade found herself being lifted off into the air in a cloud of sparkles.

Ballet Magic

The magic of the carnival music was still ringing in Jade's ears as she touched solid ground. She blinked and looked around. It felt strange suddenly being alone in the corridor at Madame Za-Za's, especially when she remembered that no time ever passed in the real world while she was in Enchantia.

Jade took a moment to compose herself then stood up tall and, with the echo of the White Cat's words in her head, she made her way back into class.

The other girls didn't notice her at first. And neither did Madame Za-Za, who was helping a group of three students with their choreography. It looked to Jade as though they were working on something quite modern. Close to them, Amber and Chloe had paired up with Amy and Lulu and the four girls had criss-crossed their arms in front of them.

They must be preparing the Dance of the Little Swans from Swan Lake, thought Jade. On the other side of the room a few people were practising dances on their own. Some looked to be working from scratch, but others were doing actual dances from real ballets.

Jade found a little space in a corner and began work on her clown dance. She smiled to herself, in her own little world, remembering her incredible adventure in Enchantia. But a moment later, when she glanced around she got a shock because the girls who had been practising the Dance of the Little Swans had stopped, and were watching Jade's clown dance. Two of them had even begun to copy the steps. And then Jade saw that they weren't the only ones copying her. All over the studio, girls had stopped what they'd been doing and seemed to be trying to learn the clown steps.

It was amazing and Jade couldn't help smiling. Her eyes met Madame Za-Za's.

"You are like a magnet, Jade!" laughed her teacher. "Your dancing is truly infectious!"

Jade laughed too. It was going to be the best Music and Dance Festival ever. She couldn't wait. It all felt just right. In fact…

…it felt magic!

*Tiptoe over the page to learn
a special dance step...*

Darcey's Magical Masterclass

First jumps

Leap for joy like the White Cat with these bouncing jumps.

1.
Start with your feet in first and your arms in preparatory position.

2.
Plié, creating the perfect diamond shape with your legs, then jump using your toes to take off.

3.
Straighten your legs and point your toes in the air, and then land softly in a *plié*.

4.
Always finish with legs straight in first and arms in preparatory position. You can repeat this jump in second position.

The Story of Petrouchka

"Come and look, the carnival is here!"

A crowd of children were running through the streets, shouting the exciting news. People pulled on their gloves and hats and rushed out into the snow to see.

The market square looked like a wonderland; there were striped circus tents, brightly-painted carousels and stall after stall piled high with golden pancakes. In one corner there was a little theatre. As the red velvet curtains were drawn back, the crowd saw three wooden puppets lying on the stage.

"Roll up! Roll up!" boomed a loud voice. "Come and see my amazing living puppets."

"They don't look very alive to me," joked a man in the crowd, and everybody laughed. But then the puppet-master started to play his magic flute and one by one the puppets sprung to their feet.

First a beautiful ballerina twirled across the stage, the sequins on her pretty pink dress sparkling in the lamplight. Next a handsome soldier leaped up. He was wearing a splendid uniform with shiny buttons. The last puppet wobbled a little bit  when he stood up. He was dressed like a clown in big baggy trousers. His name was Petrouchka.

The flute music grew louder and the puppets joined together in a lively Russian dance. They linked arms and raced across the stage, their feet moving in a blur of complicated steps. The crowd gasped. This was amazing. There were no strings holding up the puppets. They were dancing by themselves!

After the spectacular show, everyone went home happy, but inside the little theatre Petrouchka was very sad. The puppet-master had used magic to bring his puppets to life. He knew people would pay lots of money to see them. But he didn't care about Petrouchka and the others. When Petrouchka wasn't on stage he had to live in a dark 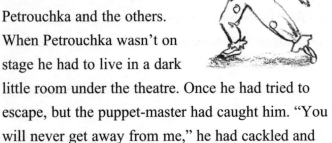 little room under the theatre. Once he had tried to escape, but the puppet-master had caught him. "You will never get away from me," he had cackled and shut the little puppet in like a prisoner.

Petrouchka heard footsteps and then the beautiful ballerina pranced into the room. "I'm bored," she said sulkily. "Do something, Petrouchka."

"Of course," stammered the little clown nervously. He was secretly in love with the ballerina and wanted to make her smile. But she was a very silly doll who only cared about looking pretty. Still, thinking it might make her happy, Petrouchka told her how he felt. The ballerina was very cross. "I could NEVER love a scruffy clown like you!" she shouted and ran out of the room.

Even though the ballerina had been horrible, Petrouchka didn't like upsetting her and wanted to say sorry. She was in the soldier's room showing off some of her dance steps, hoping the soldier would tell her how lovely she looked. But the soldier was busy looking at his own handsome face in the mirror.

The ballerina stopped mid-pirouette when she saw Petrouchka and scowled. "What do you want?" she asked nastily. "Why don't leave us alone? We were having a lovely time."

The soldier glanced up. "Yes, go away, clown," he sneered.

Suddenly Petrouchka felt angry – why were they both so horrible to him? "The soldier doesn't even like you!" he told the ballerina. "All he ever does is stare in the mirror and play with his stupid moustache!"

The soldier went very red in the face and with a

cry he chased Petrouchka from the room.

Outside, the puppet-master was returning home. He heard a shout and saw Petrouchka racing towards him looking terrified. The soldier was close behind, waving his sword.

"I'll teach you to say bad things about me," he cried, and before the puppet-master could stop him, he struck the poor little clown.

At that moment the magic seemed to disappear from both puppets and they crumpled lifelessly to the floor. The puppet-master sighed and scooped up the soldier under one arm then turned to pick up Petrouchka. He saw that the clown's wooden body was cracked open. He stood frowning down at it. "Perhaps I should just make a new clown," he thought.

"Perhaps you should," said a voice. "I won't be coming back. I'm free at last!" Slowly the puppet-master turned round and saw someone on the roof of the theatre. It looked like Petrouchka, but how could that be? The broken puppet was still lying on the floor. Suddenly the puppet-master felt frightened. Was this some sort of ghost? "Help" he cried, and he turned and ran away as fast as he could.

On the roof, Petrouchka laughed loudly. I hope that teaches him never to be unkind to his puppets again, he thought. Then the scruffy little clown took one last look at the theatre, smiled a big smile and jumped down into the snowy street to live happily ever after.

Meet other girls in Enchantia over the page…

Hello, I'm Delphie. I wasn't sure why Madame Za-Za gave me a dusty pair of red ballet shoes until they started to glow and whisked me away to Enchantia! Sugar (also known as the Sugar Plum Fairy) befriended me there and we've had lots of magic times trying to outwit King Rat and spoil his evil plans. Together we've saved enchanted guests at a masked ball, broken wicked spells and ensured the Queen's birthday show was perfect!

Hair colour: Brown

Eye colour: Blue

Likes: practising ballet excercises, Enchantia

Dislikes: King Rat

Favourite ballet: The Nutcracker

Best friend in Enchantia: Sugar

Read all my Magic Ballerina adventures...

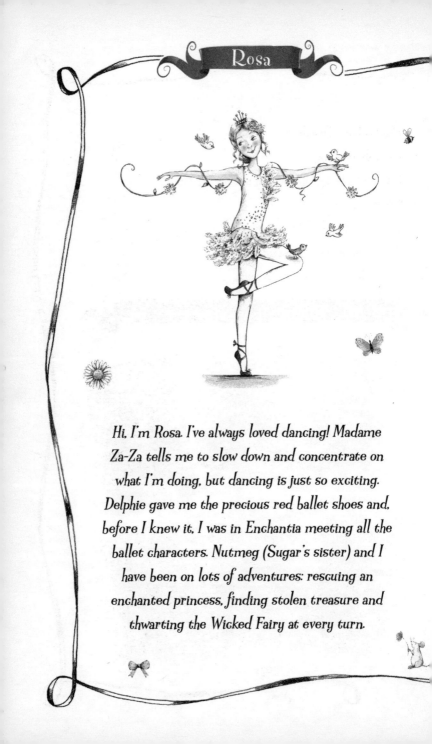

Hi, I'm Rosa. I've always loved dancing! Madame
Za-Za tells me to slow down and concentrate on
what I'm doing, but dancing is just so exciting.
Delphie gave me the precious red ballet shoes and,
before I knew it, I was in Enchantia meeting all the
ballet characters. Nutmeg (Sugar's sister) and I
have been on lots of adventures: rescuing an
enchanted princess, finding stolen treasure and
thwarting the Wicked Fairy at every turn.

Hair colour: Blonde

Eye colour: Blue

Likes: Olivia my best friend, making my mum happy

Dislikes: Making mistakes or losing my temper

Favourite ballet: Swan Lake

Best friend in Enchantia: Nutmeg

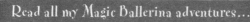

Read all my Magic Ballerina adventures…

Holly

Hi, my name's Holly and I love ballet more than anything. Dancing makes me think of my mum because she's a professional dancer. I love the emotions and stories in ballet, sometimes I get so carried away I forget where I am! Luckily I'm always in the best places: dancing at Madame Za-Za's or in Enchantia! The White Cat and I have done so much there: protecting Cinderella from an evil magician, reuniting Beauty and the Beast, and even making things right in the Land of Sweets!

Hair colour: Dark brown

Eye colour: Green

Likes: Expressing myself through dancing

Dislikes: Feeling left out

Favourite ballet: Sleeping Beauty (particularly the Rose Adagio dance)

Best friend in Enchantia: The White Cat

Read all my Magic Ballerina adventures...

The White Cat's

Magic Ballerina™

Quiz

Think you know all there is to know about
the land of Enchantia and ballet?
Well why not test your knowledge with the
White Cat's Magic Ballerina quiz!
See how many questions you can get right
and become a ballet star.

(Check your answers on page 125)

1. What colour are the magic ballet shoes that can
   take you to Enchantia?

2. What is the name of Jade's ballet teacher?

3. Who is stealing silver objects in *Jade and the
   Silver Flute*?

4. What is the famous ballet about swans called?

5. Who builds a fun fair in *Jade and the Enchanted
   Wood*?

6. What colour are the White Cat's eyes?

7. What type of dancing other than ballet does Jade like?

8. With Jade's help, who undoes the Wicked Fairy's spell in *Jade and the Surprise Party*?

9. Where do the mouse guards live?

10. What is first position with your feet in ballet?

Darcey Bussell

Buy more great Magic Ballerina books direct from
HarperCollins at 10% off recommended retail price.
FREE postage and packing in the UK.

Delphie and the Magic Ballet Shoes	ISBN 978 0 00 728607 2
Delphie and the Magic Spell	ISBN 978 0 00 728608 9
Delphie and the Masked Ball	ISBN 978 0 00 728610 2
Delphie and the Glass Slippers	ISBN 978 0 00 728617 1
Delphie and the Fairy Godmother	ISBN 978 0 00 728611 9
Delphie and the Birthday Show	ISBN 978 0 00 728612 6

All priced at £3.99

Buy more great Magic Ballerina books direct from
HarperCollins at 10% off recommended retail price.
FREE postage and packing in the UK.

All priced at £3.99

Darcey Bussell

Buy more great Magic Ballerina books direct from
HarperCollins at 10% off recommended retail price.
FREE postage and packing in the UK.

Jade and the Enchanted Wood   ISBN 978 0 00 734875 6

Jade and the Surprise Party   ISBN 978 0 00 734876 3

Jade and the Silver Flute   ISBN 978 0 00 734877 0

Jade and the Carnival   ISBN 978 0 00 734878 7

All priced at £3.99

To purchase by Visa/Mastercard/Maestro simply call
08707871724 or fax on **08707871725**